April and Ava's Adventure to Mavshi

By Eimear O'Loughlin

Illustrated by Niamh Hearty

Created by The Johnny Magory Co. Ltd

First published 2021 by The Johnny Magory Company Limited.

Ballynafagh, Prosperous, Naas, Co. Kildare, Ireland

Text and illustrations © Eimear O'Loughlin

The right of Eimear O'Loughlin to be identified as the Author of the work has been asserted by them in accordance with the Copyright Acts.

All rights reserved. No part of this publication may be reproduced, distributed, or transmitted in any form or by any means, including photocopying, recording or other electronic or mechanical methods, without the prior written permission of the publisher, except in the case of brief quotations embodied in critical reviews and certain other non-commercial uses permitted by copyright law.

Eimear O'Loughlin created this story and book following a six-week writing course during 2021 with Emma-Jane Leeson of The Johnny Magory Company Ltd.

To Mam,

Without you, this book wouldn't exist. Thank you.

Chapter One

Through the Pond

The whoosh and swish of the fresh leaves whispered in Avah's ears as she bounded through the woodlands of her native Galway. Her vision was a blur of emerald and hazel, the colours blending like swirls of paint on an artist's palette. As the wind passed through the branches of the trees, it whipped Avah's toffee-coloured hair up into a tangled mess, which fell in front of her azure-blue eyes. They peaked out from behind the soft curls that hid her pixie-shaped face, which was dotted with tiny kisses from the sun. Avah spent most of her time outdoors in the sun, when she wasn't taking care of her younger brother and sister.

As the eldest of her siblings, she took on the job of being the brave, big sister, minding and caring for them. She worked hard at home, but nature was where she could let go of any worries. The trees made her feel safe with their broad trunks and welcoming branches. So, every day whenever she got a chance, Avah would sprint from her back garden into the forest behind her house and immerse herself in the greenery which glistened against the sunlight. Avah was quite an independent child and enjoyed her freedom and peace amongst the wildlife. However, there was one other soul who Avah was very close to and who felt as connected to the earth as she did: her best friend April.

April was but twenty-two days younger than Avah, and the pair had been close since the day they met. As they got older, they unearthed their passion for nature and blossomed together. April was shyer than Avah and enjoyed the stillness that the outdoors brought as it quieted her busy mind, which buzzed constantly with worries.

While Avah was drawn to plants and flowers, the sea was April's happy place as it helped calm the noise inside her and give her space to breathe. April felt closest to herself by the waves and she wore a seashell hair clip to keep her dark hair back. The feeling of the sticky sea spray on her sun-tanned cheeks felt like coming home for April. Every day she visited the coast, collecting shells and stones the colours of a sunset. One trait both the young girls shared was their ability to find beauty in the smallest, simplest of things, like a stone or a plant which most would disregard as a weed or just a pebble.

It was this unique gift, this talent for seeing the world through grateful and curious eyes that got the two of them into the most unique situation that spring afternoon. Avah was meeting April by the forest's patch of wild bluebells and foxgloves and she was running very late, and so she took off in a hurry.

Avah eventually arrived, utterly out of breath from her sprint. Her cheeks glowed a bright magenta like she was holding a light inside her mouth. April burst out laughing at her friend's dishevelled appearance and jogged over to give her a hug. It was a Saturday, their day off school when they could explore and relax together in amongst the wildlife without any worries of homework or home. Avah had a surprise for April and had hinted all week about it in school. By the end of the week, April was anxious to find out what the big secret was!

"What do you have planned for us today, Avah?"

April asked, trying not to let Avah know that she was eaten up inside with curiosity and apprehension.

A slight smirk dimpled Avah's freckled face as she whispered, "follow the stones and you'll soon find out..."

Beyond where Avah pointed, a trail of stones and rocks dug up from the forest floor forged a path that delved deep into the thick of the trees, where all that could be seen was a descent of fog and mist shadowing the horizon. A shiver of nerves ran through April's insides like an exploding firework and a tiny gasp emerged from her lips.

However, her worries were outweighed by her mind's curiosity and so, April did as Avah said and together they journeyed along the stones. Although it was only the early afternoon, the further the girls travelled, the darker the sky became and the thicker the air grew. The click of the stones against the branches that broke under their feet punctuated their every step, the sound resounding through the forest like the cracking of bones. A swirling fog began to circle their heels, like a ghostly hand grasping at their legs. The deeper into the forest they went, April felt a tightness in her chest that almost pulled her backwards and threatened her from going any further. Now, Avah knew April inside out and could sense her anxiety before she was aware of it herself and nudged her on encouragingly.

Just as the young girls took their next step further into the blackness, a sharp glinting caught their eyes. They looked closer.

Was that... wool?

Or hair?

Its iridescence was hypnotising, the rainbowy silver-white seizing their attention. It didn't look or feel like the hair of any familiar creature native to Ireland... what was it? Where was it coming from and from whom?

April gasped as she looked down the path, excited yet afraid by what she saw, while Avah grinned and nodded at her knowingly. The hair lit up the path, bouncing off the moonlight, even though it was only two in the afternoon at home. But the girls were far, far away from there now.

A current of energy launched the girls into a run, following the glowing, flowing hair. Running and racing, Avah and April laughed as their high spirits carried them through, desperate to find out what was going to happen next. They kept going and going, until April slipped and almost tumbled into a large pond but Avah's quick reflexes saved her. The sky was a midnight black above the lake, and the darkness shrouded them like a soft, velvet blanket. The fear of being in a big dark forest alone should scare them, but something in the air made the girls feel safe. The moon came into view overhead, where the willow trees left a gaping hole. Its rays beat upon the surface of the lake, and to April's surprise, an orange, sunset glow radiated from the water.

She turned to Avah and said, amazed, "you found all of this by yourself?!"

Avah's cheeky smile exuded her pride in herself for such an achievement, "this isn't even the best part..."

Avah motioned for April to put her head in the strange water, and April looked at her like she had just grown an extra arm. Avah shrugged and, without so much as a blink, she somersaulted, headfirst, into the lake. April, now completely alone in the middle of the forest, began to freak out a bit as her anxiety from earlier came crawling back. A whisper of Avah's shadow floated under the surface and she knew then that the only thing she could do was to jump. If her best friend was going to do something ridiculous, she couldn't let her do it alone. So, she took a big breath, pinched her nose, and dived right in.

April opened her eyes and let out an astonished gasp. She couldn't believe her eyes...

Where... was she?

Chapter Two

The Alchemist and the Mavshian

A boundless landscape bursting with colour blinded Avah as she emerged from the other side of the lake. She felt a welcoming heat settle on to her skin as she passed through the water. The sun's glare pierced her eyes as she looked up into the sky, and she noticed that this was no ordinary sun and sky. In fact, it was barely a sun at all. One half was a candyfloss-pink with rays that sprouted from it like flower petals and the other was what Avah assumed to be the moon, a navy semi-circle with what looked like constellations dotting around its curved edge. They joined together, not in a full circle, but like they were passing each other by.

Curiously, there was what looked like a sapphire-coloured eye in the moon's half, and Avah felt as though its dark pupil was looking into her eyes. A little rattled, but a lot intrigued, she averted her gaze to the ground, a leafy, overgrown haven of ferns and blades and stalks, amongst other curly, spiky stems through which April appeared to be floating, transfixed by the clusters of colours. Tiny star-like formations and orbs in periwinkle blue and buttercup yellow glided through the air, which seemed to sparkle to the girls, although it may just have been their amazement at finding such a wonderland that created the glow.

Turquoise skies stretched beyond the horizon of lavender trees and vibrant, towering flowers and were filled with coral clouds which held buckets of fiery orange rain. The two strolled, hypnotised, through the wild grasslands and every now and then, they glanced at each other in pure delight and excitement.

Where in the world were they? Or were they even in the world anymore? They looked back to see if the pond from where they came was still in view and were met with an endless stretch of green. There was no sign of glittering sunset-coloured water anywhere. A faint flicker of worry passed through April as their way home had evaporated into the shimmering air, but it soon dissolved as her interest in exploring this strange place grew.

Soon, they reached a wooden signpost which appeared behind a soaring dandelion that read "MAVSHI WILDFLOWER FOREST", etched into its rough surface in a charcoal ink. The girls shared a look of eagerness, grinning widely. And through the forest the girls went!

* * *

"I wonder what time it is?" April pondered out loud.

After wandering through the forest for what felt like hours, exploring and gasping at each marvel they uncovered, the two had finally emerged and stood at its fringe. Time seemed to move faster here, and as it was beginning to grow dusky and the peacock blue sky had faded into a soft lilac haze. The twinkling call of birds filtered through the gentle breezes that combed through their hair and kissed their faces.

"Hold on..." Avah whispered, adding a harsh "SHHH!" when April asked what she was listening for.

Faintly, so indistinct it could easily go unheard, the wind carried a sweet melody in the direction of the two. It sounded as though it was being played on a harp, its tune captivating the attention of Avah who floated in its direction along a cobbled path.

Helpless but just as absorbed by the sound, April followed in Avah's steps. Behind them their shadows traipsed, staining the dips and curves of the smooth stones. Eventually they reached another signpost, similar to the one in the wildflower forest.

This one read 'Mavshi Village' where little habitats sprung from the earth as if nature created them for people or creatures. Almond-shaped doors peeped out behind vines of ivy that grew on the roofs of the peculiar homes, and the meandering streets lit up under the glow from their tiny panes of glass.

One particular building had its door swinging open, letting the plucked strings of a harp resound out on to the street, gathering a crowd of locals. Avah and April, forgetting where they were and who they were, strode confidently in the direction of the music. Gasps and some muffled shrieks arose from the cluster as the girls neared. Confusion spread across the girls' faces, Avah's forehead creasing as she realised it was they who were causing such a fuss.

One very brave member of the congregation bustled his way out and shouted with a shaking voice, "what do you think YOU'RE doing here?! Who let you into Mavshi?!"

Poor April began to tremble and just as Avah opened her mouth to retaliate and the other villagers' voices rose in fear, a towering figure appeared, looming over everyone, and hushing them into an obedient silence. The figure stood at about eight-foot-tall, intimidating with his large wooden staff and sweeping coat of midnight blue.

The local from before spluttered, "Keolin, I - ehh..."

He trailed off, shy in the presence of the giant man. Without saying a single syllable, Keolin nodded to the crowd, smiling ever so slightly, and gestured to April and Avah to follow him.

"It's April and Avah, isn't it?" he asked, turning around slightly and giving them a small smile.

Through the winding cobbled roads they went, the warm glow from the streetlights illuminating the way out of the little village and into the darkness. He stamped his staff into the ground and a fluorescent cobalt blue shone from the sphere at the top. He led them up an enormous hill that seemed to go on for miles.

The girls looked at each other, confused as they didn't know where they were going. Then, just as they were nearing the peak of the stony hill, a round hut came into view, its tapestry walls billowing in the warm breeze.

"Welcome to Jupiter Hill-Hut!" announced Keolin with a welcoming hand showing the girls inside.

It was warm like an oven, with the smell of sweet perfume heavy in the incense-filled air. A rainbow of colours flashed their eyes, with cushions and wall hangings dotted around the circular interior. Beneath the girls' weary feet, the floor was sandy and soft, and they were grateful for its pillow-like feel.

They sat down side-by-side on a magenta and ruby rug and Keolin began to talk.

"It's a pleasure to meet you both. You've had a long journey I'm sure. I'm Keolin, leader of Mavshi and the Mavshian's local alchemist. I don't suppose you know what that is?"

The girls shook their heads together with furrowed eyebrows creasing both of their foreheads.

"An alchemist," Keolin continued, "is someone with magic running through their veins. I use the earth's natural sources like gemstones and flowers to create remedies and potions for the Mavshians, if they ever are in need of my help. There are others like me, you may meet them during your time with us.

He smiled, amused by the girl's stunned silence, before continuing, "now girls, what brings you to Mavshi and what can I do to help you on your journey?"

April and Avah looked at each other, confounded.

"Uhhh... we aren't really on a *journey*..."

April began, perplexed as to what she felt she should say.

Avah took over, saying, "we fell, well *jumped*, into a pond in the forest back home that was really sparkly and pretty and we came out the other side here and we travelled through a really weird forest and we met you and -"

"Ok, ok, ok, I know how you got here, I need to know WHY you're here. What are you looking for?" Keolin quizzed.

Even more confused than before, Avah blinked, then turned towards Keolin again, serious this time.

"Myself and my friend here just came across the pond. We aren't here for anything at all! Actually, can you tell us where 'here' is?"

The giant man stood up, his head grazing the ceiling of the hut.

He inhaled deeply, and began, "Mavshi is not somewhere you will find on your maps at home. You are 'here', but Mavshi is neither 'here' nor 'there'. Those who enter our world come for a reason, to find something, to learn something. This place is here to help you discover what it is you truly seek, to awaken your mind.

You two girls want to find or learn something, even if you don't fully understand what it is you want. I am here to help you uncover what that is. This hill, this building, is named after Jupiter, the planet of growth and curiosity, of freedom and exploration. Through these things, you will find what you are looking for."

About five seconds passed before the two girls burst out in convulsions of laughter. What they were 'looking for'?! Keolin's deep, meaningful speech went over their heads and they gasped for air, breathless from laughing so hard. He gave them a puzzled look and they calmed down. He rose from his seat, standing miles above them and introduced them to one of the locals that stood with his back against the wall.

"This is Rejayd. He is going to show you around Mavshi at sunrise. Hopefully then, you will have figured out what it is you seek."

Rejayd was around the same height as the girls, like most of the villagers in Mavshi. His chestnut-coloured curly hair fell on to his shoulders, which he kept back with a scarlet bandana. He kept a mahogany guitar on a leather strap behind his back, and his light-toned skin was covered in tattoos. The inky artworks spread from his shoulders, down the length of his arms and all over his hands. At a glance, Avah noted a sun dial on the top of his hand, a music note on his thumb and another on his upper arm. It was the eye... the one in the half moon! Avah lifted her gaze sharply from his arm to meet his and he grinned at both Avah and April, clearly excited to meet them and to be their guide. Keolin and Rejayd left the girls to sleep soon after their encounter and said they would be back for them at dawn. How the tables had turned between the girls. April, normally bound up by nerves and an anxiousness to get home, lay in a deep sleep in amongst a nest of pillows and blankets while Avah remained wide awake, barely sleeping a wink. She lay tossing in her bed all night, wondering and wondering what on earth the eye meant, and why was this eye following her? Little did she know, this would soon be revealed...

Chapter Three

Stay Away from the Lake

"We've already seen the forest," April explained to Rejayd as they traipsed down Jupiter Hill and back into the village.

Avah, exhausted from her restless night, stumbled sleepily behind. Rejayd's breath became jagged as they sped up from the steepness of the hill and through shallow breaths, he began their tour of Mavshi. First, they would be meeting the Flower Sprites, a tribe of pixies who lived among the skyscraper flowers and bushes.

It seemed that Rejayd was particularly close with the little creatures, fitting right in with them in inked appearance and musical talent. Rejayd swung his guitar around from his back to his front and there they stayed for a little while, playing a few tunes that vibrated through the green stems and echoed against the hollows of the flower petals above.

The sprites had cultivated their own community within Mavshi's, and they worked hard to make their home as magical as they could. Carefully crafted buildings of tree bark were decorated with abstract paintings and colourful gemstones. That same smoky scent emanated from their houses, releasing a calming, comforting feeling into the atmosphere.

The Flower Sprites were just as interested as Keolin was about the girls' destiny and quizzed them incessantly, to which Avah and April replied with blank expressions. The sprites were cheeky little creatures and sniggered at the girls. Nonetheless, they offered their guidance and wisdom, although it felt laced with sarcasm and deviousness. Before either April or Avah could ask them what they meant by their advice, the sprites had turned back to their music and had begun to belt out another set of wild melodies. Torn between staying to join in or continuing with his task, Rejayd reluctantly tipped his head in goodbye and the three of them left the sprites in their peaceful little home.

As the trio passed by the wildflower forest, a glinting caught the girls' attention. Before Rejayd could stop them, they ran in the direction of the shimmer.

"'ANDRAYAH'S LAKE'" Avah read aloud from the scratched-up wooden signpost, which was screwed into the slippery, muddy clay that encircled the body of water. Rejayd finally caught up with them and grabbed both Avah and April's hands to drag them away. A genuine fear had lit up in his emerald eyes and he broke out in a sweat which trickled down his face.

"What's wrong?!" April asked, half-laughing at his seriousness.

"Quick, c'mon guys! You need to leave NOW!" he shouted in a panic. April and Avah looked at each other in a disappointed defeat and allowed him to drag them from the edge of the lake.

"WAIT!" April screamed and ran back. She bent down and picked up a tuft of rainbow, silver-white hair.

"Isn't this...? The hair from the forest..."

April and Avah's eyes opened wide in sudden realisation. Just as they turned to continue back to the lake, Rejayd seized their arms with force and dragged them as far as he could from the lake. When the lake was finally out of sight, Rejayd stopped and faced the pair. His usual bubbly demeanour had disappeared, and his eyes were hard and deadly serious.

"No matter how long you are here in Mavshi, don't you EVER go near that lake. Do you understand? You must listen to me. Andray- uhh... the *lake* is not safe. Ok?"

They nodded silently and they continued forward in the direction of the 'Prickly Pear Peaks'. Moments passed without a word being uttered between them as they trudged along with their heads cast down.

Just as the first mountain appeared over the horizon, Avah went to say something to April but shrieked in complete and utter terror. Rejayd turned around abruptly, his guitar swinging to his front and almost knocking him to his feet.

"WHERE IS SHE?! WHERE IS APRIL?!"

Avah felt her heart hammer against her ribcage as her vision grew dizzy and a ringing set into her ears, piercing into her skull. Where was she? Where had she gone? She stifled the instinct to cry and stiffened up, with a look of defiance and determination written all over her face.

Fear threatened to take over Rejayd too: if anything happened to this girl, how could he ever be welcomed into Mavshi again? He put his arm around Avah shoulders to comfort her, but she shrugged it off, lost in thought, trying to conjure up a plan to get April back.

Then, as he was looking in the direction from where they came, Rejayd noticed something white sparkling far beyond where they sat in the long grass. Out of sight for a human maybe, but Rejayd could just about make out what it was: the hair from Andrayah's Lake.

Determined now to find her, he reached out for Avah's hand, who took it reluctantly. They were going to follow this trail and get their friend back…before it was too late.

Chapter Four

Pink Seashells

She didn't know what compelled her to turn around, but something had gripped April's mind and before she knew what she was doing, her body swerved and headed straight for the lake. She continued to march through the long grass and suddenly, her body burst into a run and flew down the path on which they had come, a rush of blood sent straight to her head as she sped towards the lake.

Soon she arrived at the muddy banks and almost slipped into the water as she slowed her pace down from a run to a halt. The feeling inside her mind that had led her to the lake ignited once again, and April felt her arms raise to her hair to release it from her coral-pink seashell hair clip, throwing it among the spiky reeds.

She moved to the water and dipped her hand in it, creating ripples in the surface. A shuddering startled her and momentarily woke her from her trance. She watched as the ripples grew and expanded across the entire lake when suddenly, a figure began to emerge from the centre. Tall, pearly-pink skin with vines and aquatic flowers climbing up her limbs and beautiful, iridescent hair flowing from her head past her ankles and below the water. Her teal eyes locked with April's as she glided towards her, not blinking or looking away for a moment. It was like her eyes held April completely captivated and April was transfixed on this creature.

"Well... who is this we have here, trying to swim her way into my lake?"Andrayah whispered, the tone of her voice slipping through the air like water, smooth and velvety.

"I, uh.. m-my name is A-April...I-I'm s-sorry..."

"Now, now, now," Andrayah simpered, "no one ever pays me a visit... what brings you to me? What can I do for you, April?"

April stared into Andrayah's huge eyes, in awe of her ethereal beauty and spoke under her breath, "I don't k-know why I'm here, I'm so sorry f-for dis-disturbing you..."

"Well," said Andrayah, "no one can wake me unless there is something they need. You seem rattled with nerves, are you ok?"

An eruption of emotion spilled from April as her anxiety bubbled up in her chest and she began to shake from every limb. Andrayah gave her a sympathetic look but her eyes twinkled with menace. She took a step closer to April and spoke in a low voice.

"I know what you need, and I'm going to help you. Take my hand," Andrayah stretched out a bony, scaly hand to April who took it reluctantly.

"I can help you… all you need to do is trust me. Follow me now and I will show you how powerful you can become…"

April didn't quite understand what Andrayah was talking about – what 'power'? Maybe that's what Keolin meant… maybe that's what she was looking for?

Either way, Andrayah was very persuading and so, April reached out to take her hand. Petrified, April allowed Andrayah to take her deeper and deeper into the lake, until her head was all that remained above water. Andrayah turned around to smile at April, a smile that went from friendly to malicious in a flash. Before she had time to retaliate and get out of the water, Andrayah threw her arm into the air and down on to April's head, bringing her under.

*　*　*

Rejayd and Avah had been walking in silence for what felt like eternity. Avah was wrapped up in thought, her courage unfaltering. Meanwhile, Rejayd trembled inside with worry. He knew what was in that lake and feared what might have happened to April. Anything he understood about the lake he had learned from folk tales and based off those, April could be in a lot of trouble. He couldn't let Avah know any of this, though. They wouldn't worry if there was nothing to worry about, yet.

After hurrying through the track, they eventually reached the mucky, desolate clearing where the lake lay, still and sinister. The landscape was bare, the only life visible to Rejayd and Avah being themselves and the cool wind that passed through the sharp, pointed reeds at the edge of the water.

The squelch and gurgle of the sticky banks echoed their every footstep, the sound adding to the cold, miserable atmosphere that haunted the lake. The surrounding nature was almost completely devoid of colour and life. Then, out of the corner of her eye, Avah spotted something: a glimmer of hope sparked her insides as she ran towards it. April's hairclip.

She twirled it around in her hand, then looked out at the surface of the water. Something in Avah's gut told her that deep in the centre of the lake, amongst the plants and silt, is where her best friend was. Upon realising this, something shone across the still surface, so temporary she blinked twice in case she had imagined it; it was the eye. The same one in the half-moon, the same one on Rejayd's arm. A chill passed through her. Shaking it off, she and Rejayd discussed what must be done if they want to save their friend. Avah recalled Keolin mentioning something about alchemists the night herself and April arrived in Mavshi and turned to Rejayd to ask,

"Rejayd, who else here in Mavshi is magical? The way Keolin is I mean. I remember him saying there were others?"

Rejayd stopped to wonder for a moment before an idea dawned on him.

"I remember that conversation from that night and I know *exactly* who he's talking about! The Flower Sprites! Wow, how did I not think of them?! C'mon Avah, we need to go now, they'll definitely know what to do."

Motivations high, the pair left in the direction of the Flower Sprites Commune with renewed vigour.

Chapter Five

The Sprites' Elixir

A faint hum of strings and percussion bounced off the leaves as Rejayd and Avah arrived at the threshold of the Flower Sprites Commune. They brushed a large petal out of the way to see the sprites gathered around a large bonfire playing a sweet waltz that Rejayd recognised as "Lost in Quimper". The little pixies were enthralled by their own hypnotizing melody and didn't even notice the two join their afternoon revelry.

Avah tried to get the chief sprite's attention, "Eh... hello? Hi there, can you hear me? Hello? Ehmm... HIYA!"

Waving her hands frantically and shouting above the music, Avah managed to eventually meet the chief's eyes and beckon her over. A new melody had begun on a flute and she looked reluctant to leave but flew towards them anyways.

"WE NEED YOUR HELP!" Avah shouted.

The chief raised her eyebrows and gestured for her to continue.

"WELL, WE WERE PASSING BY ANDRAYAH'S LAKE EARLIER TODAY, AND WE LOST MY BEST FRIEND. WE THINK SHE - EH, HELLO? ARE YOU LISTENING TO ME? THIS IS REALLY IMPORTANT WE NEED YOUR HELP!!!"

The chief had already zoned out and was looking on at her tribe, longing to join in.

Avah's shouting snapped her back to reality as she shrieked back a "SORRY, KEEP GOING".

"MY FRIEND WAS TAKEN INTO THE LAKE AND WE NEED HELP. HOW DO WE SAVE HER?"

The sprite paused for a moment hovering in the smoky air.

"STOPPPPP!" she hollered at the other sprites. Instantly, silence fell around the commune as the music stopped.

She raised one tiny, pointed finger to her chin and thought for a moment.

"Ok... hmm... right..." The chief muttered to herself, in deep thought before a mischievous glint sparkled in her eyes.

Rejayd nudged Avah suddenly and whispered excitedly, "she's going to tell us now listen! She speaks in rhyme, so you need to pay close attention, she won't repeat it."

The chief cleared her throat and began,

"Your friend has gone missing, she's entered The Lake,

And you've come for our help, so you know what's at stake.

The creature in the water is known as Andrayah,

To retrieve your dear friend April, we know what will save her..."

Avah hung on the chief's every word, and desperately encouraged her to continue. The chief smirked cheekily, before going on:

"Before we give you any advice,

Know that our help comes at a price."

To which Avah interrupted frantically, "yes, whatever it is, I'll pay it now please help us!"

"You have been warned, now here's what to do,

Take some of these berries, yes those ones, the blue,

Mix them with petals from the sky-scraper flowers,

And add water from the lake; that will give it its power.

Now for the last, I promise it's not bad,

Drop the hair clip in, the one in your hand.

That's it! It's nearly done, look at those bubbles!

Now for your fee, I hope it's not too much trouble.

The sprite smiled menacingly at Avah, but she was paying no attention. Avah and Rejayd were both so wrapped up in the potion and getting it to their friend that they didn't hear what the chief said and made their way out of the commune. All they cared about was making sure they could rescue April. They would later find out what the price to be paid was...

Before Rejayd and Avah vanished from sight, the chief cried out to them,

"Hey! You *must* get the elixir to your friend before the eclipse is over! That leaves you with just *two* hours before the moon replaces the sun in the sky. Hurry! And don't forget our deal..."

But the two were already gone.

Chapter Six

The Lake Creature

It took Rejayd and Avah an entire hour to make it back to Andrayah's Lake and by then, the bright of the sun was dimming, casting Mavshi in an ashen haze and bringing with it a sense of foreboding. With only an hour to go, Rejayd and Avah put their worries aside and focused.

Now, at the edge of the lake, they realised they didn't actually know how to get April out. As a cloud passed by the eclipse, the remaining light from the sun lit up the water and again, Avah saw the suspicious eye. She let out a frustrated growl and, as if summoned by her annoyance, a flash of light whizzed by them to other side of the lake. A towering figure appeared from the light, so tall Avah thought it might have been...

"Keolin?!" Rejayd spurted out, answering Avah's thoughts.

They stood with their jaws gaping open as he made his way over to them, walking across the lake as if its surface was as solid as the ground surrounding it. It felt like hope had arrived just in time.

He greeted them with a slight smile and began, "I see we have a problem on our hands..."

Avah launched forward and began rambling about the disaster they found themselves in. Keolin remained silent, his reserved nature as hard to read as always.

He let her finish, paused, and spoke again, "to get April back safely from Andrayah, you will need to proceed extremely carefully. I will create a tunnel from here to the centre of the lake for you to get her Avah. Andrayah is clever, though. She will probably have her defences up to keep April from escaping, so you'll have to be crafty..."

Avah nodded slowly while glancing up at the sun – they were losing time, and they had to act fast. Keolin hammered his wooden staff into the ground and, just like before, a shining blue light burst out and reflected against the water. The water began to swirl, speeding up so fast that Avah had to look away in case she got sick. She turned back to see a dark, winding tunnel that twisted beyond, into the belly of the beast.

Rejayd grimaced at her as she stood at the gaping mouth of the tunnel. All the fears she had kept bottled up, not just from her adventures in Mavshi but from home too, rose to the surface here as she took one big breath and threw herself down the shoot. Maybe before she came to Mavshi, Avah would have passed off her anxieties with a laugh and took on the role of the fearless friend. But now, after discovering this new world, making new friends and, most importantly, having to save her best friend after losing her, Avah realised it was ok to feel a little scared. Suddenly, she felt a power surge deep inside her. She knew that feeling, and she had been suppressing it for far too long.

Anxiety. This time, she would not bottle it up – Avah harnessed herself to it, and it became her strength.

She continued to zip down the tunnel, sliding down and down and down until finally, she landed on the soft, silty lake floor. A rubbery sheen shone around her and she realised she could still breathe under the water! A gasp escaped her lips as she looked around at the dome that surrounded her and whispered to herself,

"This place just gets stranger and stranger…"

She walked forward and the vines and tentacles of the aquatic plants wrapped around her ankles and threatened to trip her up, but Avah just kicked them away, refusing to let anything stop her in her path. She looked above her and realised she was in a large bubble, its glassy curves capturing her like a spider under a glass. She called out to April, but only her voice echoed back to her. Then, a distant rumbling shook the floor and created clouds of silt and obscured Avah's vision. A dark shadow formed beyond the clouds and came slowly into view. A woman with long, white hair was coming towards her.

"Hmmm... Avah, isn't it?" Andrayah hissed silkily, as she walked forward slowly, confidently.

"Well? Where is she? Where is April?" Avah replied in a strong tone, hiding the tremble in her voice that shook her insides.

The power inside her was strong, and Avah had to control it if she wanted to get April back. A laugh flowed from Andrayah's lips as she tilted her head back and closed her eyes. She was clearly enjoying this torture.

"She's mine now! Any attempt to get her back to your precious Mavshi with all the little townsfolk and sprites and sparkles and glitter will be a waste of your time. Plus, she agreed to this... April *let* me take her..."

Andrayah's smug smirk was really beginning to irritate Avah.

A wave of anger rushed up her legs and spat out like fire from her mouth as she began to rant, "April is my best friend and there is no way I am leaving her in this rotting, pathetic lake! I will get her out and you won't be able to stop me!"

Avah charged forward and went to launch herself at Andrayah but before she could, Andrayah knelt down to the lakebed and placed both hands deep within the silt and pebbles. The floor began to quake, and vines burst through the ground and lifted Avah far up, her head almost touching the roof of the bubble.

The vines contorted around her body, stronger than she could have imagined. Avah heard Andrayah's sinister laugh from below and she was recharged with hatred. She wasn't going to let this fish-woman-creature-thing win that easily! Gathering all the strength she could, she ripped through the vines and plummeted down, landing with a resounding thud.

There were very few resources around her that she could use against Andrayah, who had disappeared from view.

'C'mon, c'mon Avah...' she muttered to herself before a brainwave hit and she grasped one of the vines that still dangled from above. Andrayah reappeared from beyond a boulder and was just about to launch a rock at Avah but she was too slow – Avah thrust the vine at Andrayah which tangled her legs together, knocking her to the floor.

Avah let out a sinister laugh of her own. But this fight was not over yet. A bubble suddenly surrounded Avah's head and as all the oxygen disappeared and was replaced with murky lake water, she began to choke. Complete terror set in as Avah shrieked in surprise.

Her screams were so loud that the bubble began to shake and wobble. Now, the entire lake floor was shuddering with the strength of her voice. The fear she felt was so real and encapsulating that Avah didn't even notice the bubble shatter and blast everything around her, battering Andrayah on to her back.

Sand flew like tornados around Avah who, through all of this, kept her eyes shut. She didn't see the sand blow away from a dark mound far from where she stood to reveal a beautiful coral shell, where her best friend lay inside, half conscious. Just as she felt her strength run out, Avah stopped shouting, and opened her eyes.

A peaceful silence met her, like one she had never heard before. She felt lighter, as this inner fear she had battled with for so long finally surfaced and ruptured out of her. Her eyes lit up when she saw April and she ran to her, forgetting too quickly where she was and the danger she was still in as Andrayah grabbed her ankle and pulled her roughly down to the ground.

She ripped one of her aquatic flowers from its roots in the sand and stamped it on Avah who watched in horror as the vines spread and tied her to the ground. Having used up all her strength in her screaming, Avah was truly trapped this time.

Andrayah rose, triumphant and before sauntering away to her cave she turned to Avah and whispered something that shook her to her core, "just another one of you to add before I can reclaim what is truly mine..."

Her long, silver hair swished behind her, and she was gone into the darkness. That silence that had felt so welcoming just moments before now felt weighted and steeped in defeat. The dome's ceiling felt closer to Avah as she lay on the ground and she felt suffocated under it, as if she was actually submersed in water. She shut her eyes as they filled with tears and felt them fall down the sides of her face and into the silt below. She felt the rocky bottom of the lake hold her as she lay there, bound up by the roots.

* * *

Rejayd paced the lake's banks up and down incessantly, completely overridden with worry, while Keolin stood like a sculpture, still and serious as he stared into the lake's surface.

"Oh no, oh no, oh no, why aren't they back yet? The elixir should've gotten them both out by now!

What do you think is going on down there ahhhh what will we do?! Keolin?!?!"

Rejayd's endless torrent of questions received no reply, so he returned to his frantic tiptoeing up and down. Minutes passed by but so slowly for the alchemist and the Mavshian as they played out scenarios in their minds while they waited for the girls' return.

Just as Rejayd had finally stopped his laps of the lake fringes, the sounds of Avah's screams burst through the water's surface and sprayed them on the shore. Keolin quickly raised his staff and directed the blue bulb at the lake, as he had done for Avah not long before. He muttered under his breath and another tunnel formed under the spell of the blinding cobalt light. Rejayd glanced between Keolin and the tunnel, his eyes darting back and forth in terror. Before lowering himself into the portal down into the lake, Keolin turned to Rejayd solemnly, nodding.

They knew that something was wrong, and that they had to go down to help the girls. And so, one after the other, they slid down the twisting slide, and landed softly on the rubble of silt and pebbles that Avah had blasted into a heap.

Rejayd felt his heart break at the sight of Avah struggling under her net of vines and April, barely conscious inside the coral shell. Their entrance had lit up the bubble dome and somewhere close, Andrayah lurked. Rejayd motioned to run over to Avah but was held back by Keolin, who knew better than to fall for the lake monster's trap. Out she came from where she was hiding, moving as smoothly as a snake towards them with a terrifyingly calm air about her.

"Long time no see, Keolin... how's life up in your little castle?" she hissed.

Rejayd took a sideways glance at Keolin, who looked as though he was wholly unbothered by these words.

Andrayah took his silence as an opportunity to continue taunting him as she went on, "and do all the little Mavshians follow you around and attend to you, idolise you and whine 'Keolin, Keolin, what would we be without you?!', like this one here?"

She nodded her head rudely in Rejayd's direction, without even looking at him. His eyes widened as he blushed and took a step away from her. Andrayah's gloating attempts to get under Keolin's skin were pointless however, as the giant shook off her words and gave her a reserved smile saying, "we would've been a great team, Andrayah. You took it too far though, and you know that. I'm sure living among these vines and murky rocks is enough of a daily reminder for you, is it?"

His smile grew daringly as Andrayah's jaw fell open before she could stop herself.

Keolin held his ground, keeping up this slight smirk while Andrayah regained her confidence.

"You talk about us being a 'great team'", she retorted, mimicking him with air quotes, "but everyone knows who the real problem was. *YOU* and your desperation to be on top, to be the 'great Keolin, leader of Mavshi'... You've warned every

Mavshian from here and beyond away from my lake, scaring them with little stories that you've twisted to make me look like the villain, when we both know that it was ME that deserves to stand where you stand, ME who deserves the recognition for Mavshi's success and YOU who should be down here in this *disgusting* lake! Look at what you've done to me, Keolin! I've had to change who I am to fit into this world you've created this *illusion* you've designed for everyone. I am not a threat to those people... *you* are."

Keolin took a deep breath and sighed slowly.

He met Andrayah's fierce but hurt eyes, and asked quietly, "why have you taken the girls...?"

Her glowering expression morphed slowly into one of sheer smugness as she responded cheekily, "now where's the fun in that...?"

The two went back and forth like this for quite some time, and Rejayd took Andrayah's distraction as an opportunity to grab Avah and April and go. Avah, exhausted from her efforts to escape and from the ordeal of it all, lay half asleep like April in the shell.

Rejayd nudged her, whispering hurriedly, "wake up, wake up, c'monnnnn Avah!" while tearing the vines from her as she slowly regained consciousness.

Just as the two moved towards April, Andrayah caught them and became unhinged with anger. Like lightening she blasted herself forward at top speed, but Keolin was quicker. He raised his staff and propelled her into her very own whirlpool.

Suspended above the lakebed she spun and spun hypnotically while she raged within it, making the water fizz and sizzle as her anger steamed from her. Quickly, the three grabbed April and made a run for the way out, fearing that somehow Andrayah would escape her turbulence and unleash her scalding-hot wrath on them.

Avah awoke from the exhausted daze instantly and she and Rejayd took April from under her arms and shot up the tunnel, leaving Keolin behind with Andrayah, still spinning.

He stood for a moment, at the mouth of the tunnel before turning to her and sighing, looking at her in genuine pity, "we could've been a great team, Andrayah... and despite the unforgivable things you've done, I still care deeply for you... you're still my dearest friend, but I have to leave you here, for your own good and for the good of Mavshi..."

Andrayah of course, heard none of this, and only caught a glimpse of Keolin as he vanished up the shoot after he released her from her watery cage. She took one sweeping glance around the wreckage that was her home, and burst into floods of tears.

Chapter Seven

The Mysterious Eye

April was sipping the elixir from its bottle when Keolin arrived back on land. They added the water from Andrayah's lake to the sprites' potion as soon as they emerged from it and watched how its sunshine gold transformed into a rich berry colour. It fizzed as April lifted the diamond bottle to her lips. She smiled. It tasted of sherbets from home.

The healing properties of the concoction were so powerful that April fell into a light snooze, lying on the banks of the lake. The group of them sat there in silence for a while, weak and worn out from the events under the water.

Seconds, minutes, possibly hours passed laying in the glorious rays of dawn. The eclipse, now fully through its cycle, had brought Mavshi through the moonlight and into the warming glow of the sun, and the four felt themselves being restored. Avah felt the muscles in her body relax finally, after being so tense from the terror of the night's events.

One thing had been eating up Avah's conscience, however: what *was* that eye? What did it mean, and why was she seeing it everywhere? She inhaled deeply before breaking the silence by calling Keolin. He gazed out over the surface of the lake which glowed under the sun in a swirling abstract of coral and yellow, before shifting his attention lazily to Avah.

"Ehh... you know when you arrived here, at the lake, before me and Rejayd went to get April? An eye appeared in the water, and I've been seeing it everywhere around here. It's even on Rejayd's arm, see?"

She pointed to her friend's upper arm, and gasped. It was gone, with no trace left behind!

Her complete bewilderment made Keolin smile to himself and chuckle, before he replied, "that eye you saw on Rejayd's arm was indeed there; you didn't imagine it. It was the same one you saw in the flowers, the lake, and the moon, wasn't it?"

Avah nodded eagerly, while her confusion and amazement grew at his all-knowing mind.

"Well," Keolin continued, "that was me. From the moment you arrived here with April, I've been looking out for you, to make sure you weren't in too much mortal peril. And what a good idea it was... You two seem to attract danger to yourselves!"

And, sure enough, Keolin's eyes shone a deep, oceanic blue, the sight of them not menacing or suspicious anymore to Avah. An immense wave of gratitude washed over her then, finally satisfied with an answer.

April began to moan and groan as she woke up. Rejayd, who had been dozing lightly through Avah and Keolin's conversation, also began to stir. The three of them watched April, anticipating a huge emotional reaction from her after being held captive and being rescued all within the space of twelve hours. Instead, she stared back at them blankly, like she hadn't a clue who they were.

The others shared concerned looks before April burst into convulsions of laughter. Her entire body trembled with her giggles and shrieks, relaxing for the first time in a long time, free from her anxiety. A glow radiated from her cheeks that were now full of their rosy pigment once again and Keolin, Rejayd and Avah let out a heavy sigh of relief, knowing that their friend April, in all her bubbly and smiley charm, had returned to them, with no harm done.

They stayed by the lake a few minutes more before it was time for the girls to return home which now, after so much time away, felt like a distant, faraway place.

Chapter Eight
A Rumble of Wings

A calming, cool breath of air billowed through the girls' hair as they made their way through Mavshi's Wildflower Forest with Keolin and Rejayd, towards the pond through which they came. The four walked in silence, regretting the goodbye that was to come.

Rejayd tried to uplift their mood with a sweet melody on the strings of guitar, which would've worked a charm had he not been disrupted by a flurry of furious buzzing that grew closer with each passing second. The iridescent sheen of wings, a blur of colour – it was the Flower Sprites, and an angry mob of them! As they neared the group, little shrieks of outrage pierced the ambient tones of the guitar and the wind.

"And where does she think she's going?!"

"Who does she think she is?!"

"The cheek of this one!"

The sprites were led by their chief who clearly saw red when she met Avah's eyes as she zoomed towards her as fast as her little wings would allow. Why she was so livid, Avah had no idea. Avah's knotted eyebrows illustrated this enough for the sprite who was nearly steaming as she began to shriek.

"Have you forgotten your promise, huh? Trying to escape, are you? You must think yourself fairly clever, thinking it would be that easy to break a promise made with a Flower Sprite! Well, NO ONE gets away *that* easy, not from me!" she shriek.

With these explosive words, she flew, headfirst, into Avah's chest and began to batter it with her tiny hands. The other sprites, under the command of their leader, flew around April, Rejayd's and

Keolin's heads, fluttering and flittering their wings in a dizzying blur.

"STOOOOOOOOOOP!"

Avah screamed, when she couldn't take another pattering from the sprite any longer.

"Why are you so angry with me? What 'promise' did I make?!"

The chief stopped, blinked, and stared into Avah's wide eyes.

"Seriously?", she said, crossing her arms and raising her eyebrows, every action laced in fiery attitude, "the elixir? You knew what was at stake. Our help comes at a price."

Avah's expression clearly stated that she hadn't an inkling what the sprite was talking about.

The chief gave her a dramatic eyeroll, before reciting,

"The price for this elixir you now have to pay,

In Mavshi, with us, eternally, you'll stay."

Silence. Ten, nine, eight... the seconds counted down slowly and Avah heard the pounding of her own heartbeat in her eardrums. A fleeting moment of recollection ignited inside her mind before escaping her again and she turned to Rejayd who had been with her during that visit to the sprites.

A shared confusion and fear felt between the two as neither recalled these particular lines. What was she going to do?! Even Keolin looked shocked. Avah moved her head to look at April, whose eyes were filling with fear. She couldn't stay here, she wouldn't. And with that stubborn nature of hers, she grabbed April's arm and ran straight for the lake.

The others responded quickly. Rejayd ran after the girls to help in their escape, while Keolin created a shield and blocked the sprites from going further beyond. He managed to stop all but one: the chief, who was now storming through the air, her wings carrying her swiftly through the sky.

Rejayd reached the lake where the girls were waiting for him, panting in an attempt to catch his breath.

"Here, take these," he gasped, handing them both a shell each, one peach and one golden.

"Use these to communicate with us over here, we're going to need your help soon I'm sure... write your message on a little scrap of paper, put it inside the shell and drop it in your side of the lake; it'll pop up here. I'll be in touch. Now go, go!"

With that, he gave them a quick hug and looked at them both with eyes full of emotion before running back to help Keolin.

The girls felt it too, but they knew they would be back. With one last backwards glance, they said a silent goodbye to their new friends and together they joined hands, held their breath, and jumped, to go back home again.

A bubbling of water, a rumble of wings,

two forces work together as one.

What does this mean, what will this bring?

Oh, the trouble has just begun...

The Characters

About the Author

Eimear O'Loughlin is a twenty-year-old from Newbridge, County Kildare. From a young age, Eimear was a prolific reader and enjoyed the wonderful, magical worlds she spent her childhood visiting. She is currently studying Music and English in Maynooth University and hopes to continue creating well into the future.

About the Illustrator

This book was illustrated by Eimear's amazingly talented auntie, Niamh Hearty. In every detail there is an ounce of magic and her passion for art and literature shines through in these beautiful illustrations.

Author's Note

Dear reader,

I really hope you enjoy escaping into Mavshi. It is inspired by a magical place in Galway, where myself and my friends stayed one summer, playing music and immersing ourselves fully in the natural beauty of Ireland's west coast.

This book makes a few nods to anxiety. For any child who holds worries inside like Avah, I hope she shows you that these fears are your strength, and you don't need to bottle them up. If you're more like April, and you feel consumed by these feelings, she is here to remind you to breathe. You are not these emotions, and you'll be ok.

Mavshi is a place I constantly revisited in my mind before it manifested into the book you're now holding. Mavshi gave me a safe haven to visit forever; let it take you to yours.

Safe travels,

Eimear x